# Chronicle of the Broken-Hearted Queen

A Crypt for my First Love

Valentine Kavardakov

Sometimes it's okay
To grieve
For longer than
You want
Pouring your emotions
Into the vase
To allow yourself
To be whole

# Warm welcome

Welcome to the grave

Where my first love lies

These are those moments

Told by a heart scorned

A heart betrayed

Navigating the complex emotions

Tied to a singular human being

# Ready

When she looked in the mirror
She saw a human ready for Love
Ready to experience
What she never had before

Unknown glory
Love mystified her
Enticed her fantasies
She could taste this feeling

She could feel the drop
As she fell for the first time
Into reciprocating arms

She was terrified
The gut wrenching feeling
Gripped her however
Excitement coursed through her

# Forbidden

Locked from her
Acceptance was key to breaking

All her life
She was told she was wrong
Secretly
How could a love so pure
Be defined as an abomination

She heard the universe speak into her
Guiding her with delicate hands
Deep within her soul she knew the truth
They were incorrect

Love is Love
Purely innocent
She would no longer be Forbidden

# Butterflies

I look upon you
Proudly
You are the one
Beating
My heart races in excitement
She loves you
With the strength
Of
A thousand suns
You delivered
Flutters
Like
Butterflies

# Smiles...

The smiles

Turn to

Laughter

Turns to

Connection

Turns to

Love

Turns to

Understood...

## ...Understood...

Turns to

Future

Turns to

Uncertainty

Turns to

Doubt

Turns to

Overthinking

Turns to

Tears

Turns to

Heartbroken.

# The Queen

She traveled the land
Delicately tearing precious petals
Lost in melancholic memories

The gusts of wind
Carried those pieces
Reminding her that nature
Always took its course

She was hopeful at times
Could visualize the silver lining
For now she had to endure
Survive the looming storms
That plagued her ravaged heart

# Fool

Am I the fool?

Am I?

The fool who loves?

Loves completely?

The fool who jumps?

Heart first?

The fool who hurts?

The fool who thinks..

And thinks..

And thinks..

And thinks..

And thinks..

And thi...................

# Haunted

Having fought for her heart

Armed with love and pure intent

Understanding his plight

Needed to convey thoughts

To try and turn the tide

Energy depleted she lies

Decaying inside till her last heartbeat

# Future//Nightmare

The smell of the flowers we planted
The sound of our pets rustling in the house
The feel of the wooden porch we wanted
The Children in the yard playing
They laugh and aren't burdened by the world

THUNDER ROARS

Her reality snaps back
She is reminded by the thunder outside
She is only daydreaming
Living the fantasy that only exists in thought
Gravely she gazes into the downpour
Tears glazing over her features
Hoping to be released from this aching misery

## Deception

You aren't who you were
She Convinced herself you loved her
Even when you didn't
She thinks you loved the idea of her

Maybe you did
In your own way
Think you loved her

From the other side
When true colors shine
Realization occurs
Ending our idealistic relationship
You are still loved by the heart you broke
That kills her inside

# Retaliation

Plant yourself Sweetie

You are a “BIG GIRL”

Maybe act like it for once

I don’t give a FUCK

But you and I know that is a lie

I would have given my last breath

For you were my home

But you didn’t care, did you ever?

Why did I not see this before

# Faintly//Loudly

She still experiences you
Her brain yearns for the idea of you
Someone who she felt understood

She knows that's not fair
You can't be what you aren't
You can only do the best you can

Next time don't let someone fight for you
Let them go sooner
Please for their sake
For hearts aren't a game
They're easily broken

## Infiltration

Do you understand
The impact of your love
Destroyed her innocence

Searched the garden inside
Slipped past her guards
You grasped her heart

Left in a flash
Taking what you needed
Discarding the rest

# Exiled

She was cast aside

Like she was a stranger to you

When she fell

Her wings were torn apart

Her heart no longer free

She plummeted into the darkness

It welcomed her with open hands

Engulfing her entirely

# Darkness

Grueling Pain

Consistent Torture

Lost in the memory and faded future

She feels as though her heart has been ripped

From the fabric of her soul

Leaving only a gapping hole in its place

She still doesn't understand the complex reason

For why she is left here alone

# Questions

How did you feel,
When you tasted her soul?

What did you experience,
When you felt her existence?

Did you drown?
Or did she?

Was the immense emotion too much?
Were you overwhelmed?

Was the universe kept inside,
To complex to understand?

Did you fail to find the beauty?
Or did she?

What did you see,
When you looked at her?

What did you feel,
When she shared her heart?

When did you know,
You moved on?

When did your heart,
Tell you it was over?

Will she ever find closure,
In the lasting silence between us?

Is this the death,
Of our blooming garden?

# Reflection

She looks at you through a reflection
Of a different timeline
When she lays alone in her bed
She see visions of you

Of us

How we never changed
How we continued to love
With everything we had

She wants to believe this is reality
But we know it isn't
You choked on your fears
Left her alone
Now I am here writing her fears
Into art to endure another day

# Final Depart

The last time we spoke

You ended us with

'I'm sorry'

With her last drop of dignity

She was able to say

'You can't fix

something you broke'

# Caress

The skin of her face remembers
Phantom caresses of your hand
Gentle glide of your lips on hers

...

Now the only thing that replaces you
Are the wet trails of pain
Dripping to the ground one by one

...

One // two // three
Drip // drop // drip // drop
Four // five // six

# Cold

Chilled

In the frozen wasteland

Of her locked mind

All of this was viciously real

She felt every pulse of your truth

She felt the realness of our opposition

She would rather embrace the void in DEATH

Than to live in the lie you made for her

## Universe of Reality

She used to feel
The universe guide her
Was gifted something beautiful
Just to experience this
Decay and destruction
Of the very gift given to her

The alluring touch of a wise teacher
She trusted immediately what they implied
Forgetting entirely what she knew
The universe often has two faces
One that gives opportunity
And
One that watches fate

# Unlike Me

I don't want this

I don't just give up

I pinkie promised I would be present

I would rather sacrifice virtues

Or my sanity

I don't give up

I can't get over you

....

No not yet

## ¿Acceptance?

Sometimes
She
would
Rather
Be
A
**Fool**
Than
Not
Have
Loved
At
All

# Is This Moving On

She

Realizes the pain needs to go

Slowly

She's felt it enough

Though

She will always remember

She

Wants the future

Now

More than ever

# Her Kingdom

When

The Chaotic Princess

Sings

She reminds herself

That

She is the ruler

Of

Her own kingdom

And

Not one human

Can

Take that away

Ever

# Growth

What she did not know

At the time

Was that growth

Always starts in the dark

Just like the seed

In darkness we thrive

To be better to ourselves

## Double Edge

Love is

The double edged blade

That sets humans apart

We just abuse the concept

It all comes back to control

For humans crave power

Doing anything to maintain the mantle

## ...HeartBroken...

Turns to

Pain

Turns to

Endless waterfalls

Turns to

Misunderstanding

Turns to

Begging

Turns to....

# ...Abandonment...

Turns to

Questioning

Turns to

Triggers

Turns to

Breathing

Turns to

Clarity

Turns to....

## Blank

I awoke
To see nothing
There exists nothing
Nothing
Absolutely empty
Needing a creative author
Blank
An expression
Blank
A statement
Blank
An issue
Blank
Isn't really blank
It is just clear art
To be seen by those
Who pay attention

## Clear

Empty
She is depleted
She had given
Her heart
Made herself invisible
Hiding her traits
Wants and needs
To spare the one she loved
Her rose colored glasses
Now remain shattered
The raw truth
Stared back at her
She had become
Clear
Leaving her
In this blank space
Desolate

# Faint Kiss

The Kiss of Someone else

Tastes foreign

Feels alien

Is different

You left your fingerprints on her

Reminded of what she gave you

The first sensual touch she had ever given

Was yours

She will forget you that's a promise

# Breathe

The fresh air

Is intoxicating

Soothes the burns

Throughout her chest

Feeling the energy swirling

Moving in and out

In and out

Letting go the past

One breath at a time

# Deserve

She deserved better

Her king will arrive

Interestingly enough  she will find

Him within herself

For she is the ruler

Of herself and her energy

She is POWER

She is the prismatic explosion

That will rid herself of you

# Convergence

As time progressed
She has noticed the shards of her heart
The ones that were buried in the ashes
Start to tremble and move
Ever so slightly
The vibrations have elevated
Responding to her call
Her intention to be whole again

Watered by her tears
She will reclaim what is hers
Returning back to who she was
Never to be forgotten
She will flourish
Become renewed
Taking back her
Fucking Kingdom

# Beautiful Stranger

She looked in the mirror

Her reflection had changed

The scars of battles waged

Lie upon her complexion

The dark circles from restless nights

Are enough to make a stranger wonder

# Pride

As she gazes at this woman

She is filled with pride

Proud to survive

Proud of the scars and dark circles

She is well aware that these signs

Prove she lives to fight another day

# Magik

She is composed of ancient magik

Tightly wound strings in an orchestra

Tides both great and small

Gusts chaotic and gentle

She is an enigma

Brave and Scared

Watch her become

The Ethereal Goddess

## ...Understanding.

Turns to

Smiles

Turns to

Laughter

Turns to

Unconditional Love

Turns to

Becoming Whole Again

# Finer Things

Life is speckled with delicate strands of light

These live in memories tucked softly away

They reside within the sensual caress of a kiss

Hidden in the lasting embrace of a lover

They can be found within the clear open sky

## Reprise

The finer things sometimes are the only motivation

To continue on this hike through life

We should cherish the little moments of joy

Witness their existence in honor

Cause once our clock stops ticking

All that will remain

Are

The Finer Things

# Ascension

When the distractions subside

She will climb

Reaching new peaks of self actualization

Here she is reminded

No man

Could ever stand in her way

Again

# Underlying Truth

There are secrets everywhere

One truth always speaks loudest

Self love can mend broken hearts

She will fix what was lost

By her Fucking self

Stand clear

She doesn't need you anymore

# Unknown

What she found in the crevices
Of her heart
Was a written particular secret
She knew all along

Hidden in her
Was an immense energy
That when embraced
Burst in full emotion

# Butterfly

I am the truth
A cosmic evolution
Floating within enigmatic energy

Guided by the mistress
She is the universe
She anchors my sanity
Embraces my flaws

I am HER butterfly
Having transformed before HER eyes
I am beautiful
In every single moment

## Thankful

I am truly grateful

For those who stood by

Who embraced me in my darkness

Who showed me

What it means to love

Who supported me

Through my many spirals

I love you all

Sincerely Forever

# Free

Crisp Night Air

Bright Gleaming Moon

Restful Silence Pursues

Clear Thoughts Flow

Finally

Understanding Myself

• • •

•

•

•

•

The queen
Still travels
She's lived on after these events
Going on to fuel her creative
She released this work
Extremely personal confessional
Though after time passes
She relives these moments
And from that new ideas form
From old places
So she opens the book once more
And adds to the complexities
Because the story
Is never truly over

•

•

## Or so I thought

After many nights spent
Time has scabbed the wound
She still feels the pain
But it's okay now

She knows herself more now than ever
She's happy for the time
Spent alone on these quiet nights

New realizations came along the way
She wasn't perfect
That's a given however
She understands this road
Is never easy for anyone

# 2 long years

It's tough to imagine
Such an integral part of her life
Has died so long ago

Shit still remains present in her life
She feels fucking stuck for no goddamn reason
The 3 months felt so long for her

She wonders often
If she's just a distant memory for him now
Or by chance does she cross his mind just the same

She may never know
But regardless
She hopes he is happy

# Life goes on

She continues on
Never taking herself for granted
Boy after boy

Entertaining others
Searching for connection

400 or so boys later
Still not one worth her time
Endless good mornings and last goodbyes

Her past still calls
New words form for old wounds

She will share them with you
Just you wait

# Poison Apple

The anticipation sparked her craving
Hesitation persisted but
She cracked and took a bite

He was sickly sweet with a layer of sour
That danced along her tastebuds
Teaching her new sides of her senses

She loved every moment
Holding the apple closer than ever
Not aware of the fact it would be her downfall

Getting her fill every time
He fed her and she fed him
Dazzling experiences and new love

She consumed so much of him
She lost herself in the story of first loves heartbreak

# OnLine Dating

Pleasant introductions

(Could this be it?)

Dedicated conversations

(Are her butterflies waking up?)

Revealing sensual moments

(Is she attractive to them?)

Mutual confessions of affection

(Silent excitement)

Growing distant suddenly

(Where did he go?)

No response left on read

(Why does this always happen)

?¿?¿?

## Mental audience

She mocks conversations in her head

"How can I speak to him?"
"Easy, I do it all the time"

She speaks to the memory of him
The one stuck firmly on the permanent timeline

Existing only for her
In her loneliest of times

*Long...Lost...Love*

# Him

Not gonna lie

I thought I could

Call you always

Keeping you at the center

Going so far as to

Leave myself behind

I never would have imagined

Couldn't have been expected to

Know you would break me

She felt it all

The things spoken aloud

Tore her to pieces

You couldn't do this

She gave her sanity for you

All because you asked

# Retrospective Limelight

Maybe her deciding to love someone
Just as damaged as her
Was a bad call

She never noticed the double standards
Being told upfront
He would never put anyone first again

Should have been the first red flag
She as an empath completely understood

Her as the abandoned project
Would never ever understand

# Repetition

Writing circles

Years later

As if

Moving on

Can't happen

For someone

Like her

Anyone who harms her

Lives cemented in the folds of her brain

As if she tortures herself

With everyone she has ever loved

Sitting there looking upon with

Disapproval and knowing

She was never going to be good enough

For them

# Better for it

As she sits here
Sharing the tiniest of details
You don't have to know

She wants to share with you
That for her it's never really over
Healing is messy as shit

She used to wonder why it took
Some humans years and years
To move along with their lives

She knows now
First hand that it isn't that simple
The dichotomy of never wanting this to have happened
And being better for it all the same
Lives wildly in her now

## Butterfly II

She learns from the truth
She could never be perfect
The universe doesn't own her

She once grew for the universe
Time has shown
She does this on her own

No higher power was responsible
Her healing is done to her own credit
The mistress has no place here

She has been beautiful all along
She didn't need the universe
She just needed to accept her place in it
We are all stardust and return all the same
Let that be enough for you

# Royalty

She is good enough
Just because things didn't work out
Does not limit her self worth

Wrong place / wrong time

Whatever it may be
she chooses
To love on

The important ones stick around
That is the secret
Be confident in the experience
Change with the seasons
Just simply enjoy being

*HUMAN*

# This is the End

The Broken-Hearted Queen
Shares her story with the world
Open and vulnerable
So you can feel her authenticity

Understand the road she paved
She walks everyday this rough path
In the concept of time
As she gazes up towards the stars

The magik swirling above
Will always be there

She will rest finally
And those along the way
We're just pages to be turned
So she can continue to write the future she deserves

# Dreaming

A single full tear for the one she lost
To the endless waterfall of time

She will always remember you
The ways she loved you and you her
Every piercing emotion
That you brought to her attention

Be set free
To the rolling sands
She has to move along
She has new dreams to follow
And you're holding her back
Lay to rest in this tome

*Rest in peace my love*
*My one and only*

*Thank you again*

*For taking the time*

*To delve into my story*

*May you feel seen*

*May you feel loved*

*-Val*

*-XOXO-*

*Always and forever*

*Isn't as long as I thought it was*

www.ingramcontent.com/pod-product-compliance
Lightning Source LLC
LaVergne TN
LVHW091227150826
845673LV00003B/1049

* 9 7 9 8 3 5 4 8 6 9 4 1 1 *